The Nutcracker

E.T.A. HOFFMANN

Illustrated by
SANNA ANNUKKA

Adapted from the translation of
MRS ST SIMON

HUTCHINSON

1 3 5 7 9 10 8 6 4 2

Hutchinson
20 Vauxhall Bridge Road
London SW1V 2SA

Hutchinson is part of the Penguin Random House group of companies
whose addresses can be found at global.penguinrandomhouse.com

Illustration copyright © Sanna Annukka 2017

First published in Great Britain by Hutchinson in 2017

\   www.penguin.co.uk

A CIP catalogue record for this book is available from the British Library.

ISBN 9781786330635

Typeset in 11/13.2 pt Bodoni Seventytwo ITC by Jouve (UK), Milton Keynes
Printed and bound in Italy by Graphicom Srl

Penguin Random House is committed to a sustainable future
for our business, our readers and our planet. This book is made
from Forest Stewardship Council® certified paper.

FOR
BETHAN & NOAH

CHRISTMAS EVE

During the long, long day of the twenty-fourth of December, the children of Doctor Stahlbaum were forbidden from entering the parlour. Fritz and Marie nestled together in the back chamber as dusky twilight came on. In hushed tones Fritz was telling his little sister that he had not long before seen a little dark man glide along the corridor with a large box under his arm, but he knew full well that it was only Godfather Drosselmeier. At this Marie clapped her little hands for joy and exclaimed, 'Oh what do you imagine Godfather Drosselmeier has made for us this time?'

Counsellor Drosselmeier was in no way a handsome man. He was small and thin with a wrinkled face and a large black patch over his right eye. To cover his bald head he wore a lovely white wig made of glass. It was a rather ingenious artefact. But then, the Godfather was a rather ingenious man himself, for he knew all there was to know about clocks and how to make them. When one of the many beautiful clocks in Doctor Stahlbaum's house was sick and could not sing, Godfather Drosselmeier would come and pierce it with all manner of sharp instruments. This always made Marie quite anxious, but it did the clock no harm; on the contrary, it would become quite lively again, striking and singing so merrily that it was a pleasure to all who heard it.

henever he visited he had a little something in his pocket for the children, but when he arrived on Christmas Eve he brought a gift of such splendour that their parents would always put it away for safekeeping afterwards.

Fritz thought that this time it would be a castle, patrolled by many fine soldiers, who would defend it with their cannon fire when it was under siege.

'No, no,' Marie interrupted him, 'Godfather Drosselmeier told me about a lovely garden with a great lake and the most beautiful swans which sing sweet songs. Then a little girl comes along and feeds them marzipan.'

'Swans don't eat marzipan,' scoffed Fritz, 'and even Godfather Drosselmeier can't make a whole garden. Besides, his toys aren't much good if they are always taken away from us again. I like our gifts from Papa and Mama much better, for we can keep those and do with them as we please.'

Just at that moment there was the silvery *cling, ling* of a bell and the doors flew open to reveal a dazzling light from the parlour. The children's parents appeared at the doorway and, taking them by the hand, said, 'Come, children, and see what Christmas has brought you this year.'

The children must have been very good that past year, for never before had they received so many fine presents. In the centre of the room there stood a magnificent fir tree decked with gold and silver apples, while sugar almonds and lemon drops adorned its branches like buds and blossom. All around the tree were laid the most beautiful gifts of every description. Marie spied the daintiest dolls, a tea set and all sorts of little trinkets. Fritz went straight to his new regiment of hussars, who were most handsomely clad in red and gold and looked very smart indeed on their white horses.

The children had just turned to some exquisitely-drawn picture books, when – *cling, ling* – the bell sounded again. This was a sign that Godfather Drosselmeier would now reveal his gift and so they ran to the table where their godfather's present was concealed by a long velvet curtain. Imagine their delight when the curtain was drawn aside!

magnificent castle stood on a lush green lawn covered with flowers. Its golden turrets shone brightly and the light gleamed on its clear glass windows. A bell sounded inside the castle and the doors and windows flew open to reveal scores of little men and women going about the many rooms. The great hall was aglow with the light of a thousand tiny candles and children in white dresses and green jackets could be seen dancing to the music. At intervals a man in an emerald-green cloak appeared at the window, waved and promptly disappeared again. And every so often Godfather Drosselmeier himself – though he was hardly bigger than their father's thumb – emerged at the door of the castle to wave at the children.

Fritz watched the scene, his chin resting on his hands, before saying, 'Godfather Drosselmeier, let *me* go into your castle.' The Counsellor gave him to understand that this could not be done. And indeed it was most foolish of Fritz to wish to enter a castle barely as tall as he was.

After Fritz had watched the ladies and gentlemen, and the dancing children and the emerald man at the window and Godfather Drosselmeier at the door for some time, he cried out impatiently, 'Let the green man at the window walk about with the rest.'

'That cannot be done either,' said the Counsellor.

'Then the children must come down so I can see them better.'

'None of that can be done,' replied the Counsellor, curtly. 'As the mechanism is made, so it must remain.'

'Well then, Godfather Drosselmeier,' said Fritz, 'if that's how it is then I don't think much of your little figures in the castle. My hussars are far better, for they can go back and forth as I order them.'

And with that he turned his back on Godfather Drosselmeier's creation. Marie had also slipped away because she too found the scene tedious after a while but, unlike her brother, was too polite to say so.

'An ingenious work like this was not made for silly children,' snapped Counsellor Drosselmeier angrily. 'I shall pack up my castle and take it home.'

But then their mother entreated him to show her the curious mechanism by which it all worked, and so the Counsellor took the whole thing apart and put it back together again. This put him into good spirits once again and he gave the children some little men and women with gilded faces which smelled like sweet gingerbread. Fritz and Marie were very pleased with them indeed.

Just at that moment Marie spotted something which nobody else had yet noticed. At the back of the table was a curious little man, standing quietly, as if patiently awaiting his turn. He could not be called a handsome man, for not only was his rather stout body out of all proportion to his spindly legs, but his head was altogether too large for either. But it was clear that he was a man of taste and education, for he wore a hussar's jacket of beautiful bright violet with matching pantaloons and the neatest boots you ever did see. He also had on a somewhat clumsy wooden cloak and a woodman's cap. These last two made him look a little ridiculous if the truth be told, but Marie remembered that Godfather Drosselmeier's cap and cloak were equally shabby, and he was still a dear godfather. In fact, the longer she looked, the more kindness and benevolence she saw in the little man's clear green eyes.

'Papa,' exclaimed Marie at last, 'to whom belongs that charming little man by the tree there?'

'To both you and Fritz,' said her father. 'And he shall work hard for you, for he can crack the hardest nuts with his teeth.'

ery carefully her father took Nutcracker and lifted his wooden cloak, whereupon the little man opened his mouth wide to reveal two rows of sharp white teeth. At her father's bidding Marie popped a nut into the little man's mouth, and – *crack* – the shell fell away, and she caught the sweet kernel in her hand.

'This little fellow,' Dr Stahlbaum explained, 'comes from a long line of Nutcrackers and practises the profession of his forefathers. Since friend Nutcracker is such a favourite with you, Marie, I place him under your care, though Fritz shall have just as much right to his services.'

Taking Nutcracker in her arms, Marie immediately set him to work cracking nuts. She picked only the smallest, however, so that he wouldn't have to open his mouth too wide, which was not overly becoming. In the meantime Fritz had tired of his hussars and come over to investigate. He laughed heartily at the funny little man and began to choose the biggest and hardest nuts for him to crack. Then all at once – *crack* – out fell three of Nutcracker's teeth, and his jaw became loose and rickety.

'My poor Nutcracker!' cried Marie, and snatched him from Fritz's hands.

'Stupid fellow,' said Fritz. 'He wants to crack nuts with poor teeth – he doesn't understand his trade. Give him here, Marie. He shall crack nuts for me even if he loses all his teeth.'

'No, no,' wept Marie, 'you shall not have my dear Nutcracker. See how sorrowful he looks!'

Crying bitterly, she wrapped the injured Nutcracker as quickly as she could in her pocket handkerchief. Just then their parents arrived with Godfather Drosselmeier who, to Marie's dismay, sided with Fritz. But Dr Stahlbaum said, 'I have placed Nutcracker under Marie's protection, and as I see that he is now greatly in need of it, I give her full authority over him. I am surprised at Fritz. A good soldier ought to know that those wounded in service are not expected to fight.'

Fritz was rather ashamed of himself and, without a further thought of nuts or nutcrackers, stole back to his hussars. Marie collected Nutcracker's lost teeth and tied up his wounded chin with a nice white ribbon. He looked so pale and frightened that she wrapped him all the tighter in the handkerchief.

Contrary to her usual disposition, Marie became quite cross with Godfather Drosselmeier at dinner when he laughingly asked why she cared for such an ugly little fellow. Remembering that odd similarity between Nutcracker and Drosselmeier, she said very seriously: 'I'm not sure you would be as handsome as Nutcracker, Godfather, if you were dressed as finely as he and wearing such bright little boots!' Marie could not understand why her parents laughed so loudly at this or why the Counsellor's face turned red and he did not laugh half so heartily as he had before.

In the sitting-room of Doctor Stahlbaum's house there stood a high glass case, in which the children kept all the beautiful things given to them every year. On the upper shelf, too high for Marie and Fritz to reach, all Godfather Drosselmeier's curious machines were kept. Immediately below this was a shelf for the picture books; the two lower shelves Marie and Fritz filled up as they pleased, but it always happened that Marie housed her dolls on the lower shelf, while Fritz stationed his troops on the one above.

And so that evening, while Fritz set his hussars in order above, Maria installed the new doll in the best furnished chamber below and invited herself to tea with her. It really was a well-furnished room, with a lovely chintz sofa and several dainty chairs, a finely arranged tea table, and a little bed with crisp white sheets. The new doll, Miss Clara, was quite comfortable that evening.

It was now quite late and Godfather Drosselmeier had long since gone home, yet still the children could not leave the glass case, although their mother repeatedly told them that it was high time they went to bed.

'It is true,' cried Fritz at last; 'my poor hussars would like to get some rest but won't dare nod off as long as I am here.'

And off he went to bed, but Marie pleaded, 'Just a little longer, Mama. I have one or two things to attend to, and once they are done I will go straight to bed.'

Marie was a very sensible child, so her mother could leave her alone without anxiety. But in case she was so distracted with her new doll that she forgot to put out the lights, Mrs Stahlbaum extinguished all the candles save for one, which cast a soft, pleasant glow.

'Come up soon, my dear, or you will not be up in time tomorrow morning,' called her mother, as she went up to bed.

As soon as she found herself alone, Marie took out the wounded Nutcracker from her pocket and, laying him carefully upon the table, unrolled the handkerchief gently, and examined his wound.

'Nutcracker, do not be angry at Fritz for hurting you so, he did not mean to be so rough; it is the wild soldier's life that has made him a little hard-hearted, but otherwise he is a good fellow, I can assure you. Now I will tend you very carefully until you are well again, though Godfather Drosselmeier will have to fix your teeth: he understands such things.'

But Marie was hardly able to finish the sentence, for as she mentioned the name of Drosselmeier, Nutcracker made a terrible wry face, and sparks flashed from his green eyes. Marie was quite alarmed until she saw it was only the sad smiling face of the honest Nutcracker before her, and she knew that it must have been the glare of the lamp which had distorted Nutcracker's features so strangely. 'What a foolish girl I am,' she said, 'to be so easily frightened, and to think that a wooden doll could make faces at me.'

ith this Marie took her friend the Nutcracker in her arms, carried him to the glass case and said to her new doll, ' Miss Clara, please be so good as to give up your bed to the wounded Nutcracker, and do as well as you can with the sofa.'

Miss Clara looked very grand and haughty, and said nothing at all. 'What other arrangements can we make?' wondered Marie, and she laid little Nutcracker gently on the bed, draped a ribbon from her dress around his poor shoulders and tucked him in.

'He shan't stay with the naughty Clara,' she said, and placed the bed with Nutcracker in it on the shelf above with Fritz's hussars.

She locked the case, and was about to go up to bed, when quite suddenly she heard a strange whispering and rustling all around her. The great clock whirred louder and when Marie turned towards it she saw that the large gilt owl perched on the top had dropped down its wings so that they covered the whole clock face. And the clock whirred louder until it seemed to be saying:

'Hickory, dickory, dock – whir softly clock – Mouse King has a fine ear – pum pum the old song let him hear – prr – prr – pum – pum – dong ding, little bell ring – sound and send him packing.'

rembling with fear, Marie was on the point of fleeing when she saw that the owl on the clock was none other than Godfather Drosselmeier, who had let the flaps of his coat hang down like wings. Plucking up her courage, she cried: 'What are you doing up there, Godfather Drosselmeier? Come down, and do not frighten me so, you naughty Godfather Drosselmeier!'

Just then a wild squeaking and scuttling broke out all around her, and Marie could hear a strange pattering noise, as though a thousand little feet were in motion. Then, quite suddenly, a thousand tiny lights appeared through the cracks in the floorboards. But as Marie looked closer she saw that they were not lights – they were eyes. Crawling out of every nook and cranny were hundreds and hundreds of mice. Now Marie was not afraid of mice as most children are, and she was just thinking that they were even a little amusing, when all at once there arose a squeaking so terrible that it sent shivers down her spine.

Close before her feet there burst out of the floorboards seven mouse heads, and each head was adorned with a glittering crown. Then arose the one mouse body to which these seven heads belonged, and the great Mouse King advanced to meet his army with an almighty squeak. At once the rank and file began to march forward, straight towards the glass case, and poor Marie who stood before it!

er heart had been pounding so forcefully before that she feared it might leap out of her chest, but now her blood seemed to run still in her veins. Half in a swoon, she tottered backward, when *clatter* – her elbow struck a glass pane and it fell in pieces at her feet. She felt at that moment a sharp pain in her left arm, but then her heart lifted as she heard a little voice from inside the glass case:

'Up, up, awake – arms take – awake – to the fight – this night – up, up – to the fight.'

And now, Nutcracker had leaped out of bed and was shouting:

'Crack – crack – stupid pack – drive mouse back – stupid pack – crack – crack – mouse – back – crick – crack – stupid pack.' With these words he drew his little sword, brandished it and exclaimed, 'My loving vassals, friends and brothers, will you stand by me in the hard fight?'

Three scaramouches, a harlequin, four chimneysweeps, two guitar-players and a drummer immediately cried out, 'Yes, my lord, we will follow you with fidelity and courage – to victory or to death,' and they rushed after the fiery Nutcracker to venture the dangerous leap down from the upper shelf.

It was easy enough for them to perform this feat, for their insides were made of cotton and straw so that they landed on the floor like soft packs of wool. But Nutcracker would certainly have broken his arms or his legs, for it was almost two feet from the shelf to the floor, and his body was as brittle as linden wood. Yes, Nutcracker would certainly have broken his arms or his legs, if, at the moment when he leaped, Miss Clara had not sprung from the sofa, and caught him in her soft arms.

'Oh good Clara,' sobbed Maria, 'how I have wronged you! You were no doubt very happy to give up your bed to little Nutcracker.'

Now Miss Clara spoke, pressing the young hero to her silken bosom. 'I beg you, my lord! Do not, sick and wounded as you are, share the dangers of the fight. See how your brave vassals assemble themselves, eager for the affray and certain of conquest. Will you not rest upon the sofa, or from my arms look down upon your victory?'

But Nutcracker was struggling so violently that Clara was obliged to set him down. He then, however, dropped gracefully upon one knee, and said, 'Fair lady, the recollection of your kindness will go with me into battle.'

lara then took him by the arm, removed her sash and was about to drape it across Nutcracker's shoulders when he stepped two paces backward, laid his hand upon his breast, and said very earnestly, 'Do not lavish your favours upon me, fair lady, for –' He stopped, sighed heavily, tore Maria's ribbon from his shoulders, pressed it to his lips and let it hang down like a field bandage. Then with a flourish of his sword, he leaped nimbly from the lower shelf to the floor. For Nutcracker, even before he had come to life, had felt Marie's kindness and love, so that he preferred to wear her simple ribbon than Miss Clara's sparkling sash.

As soon as Nutcracker had leaped out, the squeaking was heard again. Under the large table the hateful mice were concealed in their thousands, and high above them all towered the dreadful mouse with seven heads! What will happen next?

'Beat the battle march, true vassal Drummer!' cried Nutcracker and immediately the drummer began to drum furiously so that the windows of the glass case trembled and then Marie saw that Fritz's soldiers were leaping from their boxes and hurrying into formation on the bottom shelf.

Then Nutcracker turned to Harlequin and said earnestly, 'General, I know your courage and your experience; there is need now for a quick eye, and skill, to seize the proper moment. I entrust to your command all the cavalry and artillery.'

Thereupon Harlequin put his long, thin fingers to his mouth, and crowed so piercingly that he sounded like a hundred shrill trumpets. Then much whinnying and stamping was heard from the glass case and out marched Fritz's cuirassiers, dragoons and his splendid new hussars.

egiment after regiment now lined up in long rows on the floor before Nutcracker. The cannons went first and — *boom* — sugar-plums were fired into the army of mice, covering them in white powder and throwing them into disorder.

Yet the mice continued to advance, and some even overcame the cannons, but by this time there was so much smoke and dust that Marie could hardly see what was happening. What was clear, however, was that the battle had become fierce and a victor by no means certain.

Above the chaos, the cries of Miss Clara could be heard, who was running every which way in panic, crying, 'Must I die in the blossom of youth?'

The mice were ever increasing in number and their gunfire rained upon the glass case. Nutcracker strode through the ranks of Fritz's hussars, giving the necessary orders and encouragement to the troops. But whilst Harlequin had led the cavalry admirably, the hussars had been battered by the enemy's odious fire, and so had halted their advance. Harlequin ordered them to draw off to the left, and in the enthusiasm of command, headed the movement himself. The entire cavalry followed, and so they all headed for home. This left the cannons exposed to the ambush of some very ugly mice and so they too were lost.

Nutcracker, now completely surrounded by the foe, was in the greatest peril. He tried to leap over the edge of the shelf and into the safety of the glass case, but found his legs too short. Clara lay in a great swoon so could not help him and at that moment two mice took hold of his wooden mantel. The Mouse King, squeaking with all seven heads, leaped in triumph towards him and Marie could no longer control herself. 'Oh, my poor Nutcracker!' she cried, sobbing, and without being exactly conscious of what she was doing, grasped her left shoe, and threw it with all her strength into the fray, straight at the King. In an instant the mice had scattered, but Marie felt in her left arm a still sharper pain than before, and sank unconscious to the floor.

When Marie woke, she found herself lying in her own bed, with the sun shining bright and sparkling through the ice-covered windows. Close beside her sat a stranger, whom she soon recognized, however, as the Surgeon Wendelstern.

He said softly, 'She is awake!' Her mother then came to her bedside and looked at her anxiously.

'Are all the mice gone, Mama?' lisped little Marie, 'and is Nutcracker safe?'

'Do not talk such nonsense,' replied her mother. 'You naughty child, you have caused us a great deal of anxiety. You played until very late last night and you became sleepy, probably, and a mouse may have jumped out and frightened you. In any case you fell and pushed your elbow through the glass and cut your arm very badly. Neighbour Wendelstern, who has just removed the piece of glass from your arm, says that you might have cut an artery and bled to death. It was fortunate that I woke about midnight and saw that you were not in bed. I found you in front of the toy cabinet, bleeding profusely and surrounded by Fritz's soldiers, broken china figures and one of your shoes.'

'But Mama,' interrupted Marie, 'those were the traces of that dreadful battle between the dolls and the mice. And the mice were going to take poor Nutcracker prisoner so I threw my shoe at them.'

Surgeon Wendelstern gave the mother a look, and she said very gently to Marie, 'Well, never mind about it now, my dear. The mice are all gone and little Nutcracker is safe and sound in the glass case.' Doctor Stahlbaum now entered the chamber, spoke for a while with Surgeon Wendelstern, and then felt Maria's pulse. She heard him say something about a fever and that she should stay in bed for a few days. She did, although, other than a slight pain in her arm, she felt quite well and comfortable. Occasionally she thought she heard Nutcracker's voice calling to her. 'I owe you great thanks, dear Marie. But there is still something you could do for me.' But Marie could not imagine what it might be.

She could not play very well on account of her injured arm, and when she tried to read, a strange glare came across her eyes, so that she was obliged to desist. The days seemed endless and she waited impatiently for evening, when her mother would come to tell her a story.

One evening her mother had just finished a story when the door opened, and in came Godfather Drosselmeier. As soon as Marie saw him in his brown coat, she remembered the night of the battle and she cried out, 'Oh Godfather Drosselmeier, you have been very naughty; I saw you cover the clock with your wings, so that it should not strike loud and scare away the mice. Why did you not come to help poor Nutcracker and me?'

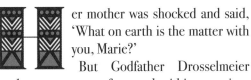er mother was shocked and said, 'What on earth is the matter with you, Marie?'

But Godfather Drosselmeier made a very strange face, and said in a grating, monotonous tone: 'Pendulum must whirr – this way – that way – clock will strike – tired of ticking – all the day – kling – klang – bang – bing – 'twill scare away the Mouse King.'

Maria stared at Godfather Drosselmeier. He looked far uglier than usual and moved his right arm back and forth like a puppet on strings. She would have been afraid of him if her mother had not been present, and if Fritz had not slipped in and laughingly interrupted him. 'Ha, ha! Godfather Drosselmeier,' he cried, 'you are too funny today!'

But their mother was very serious, and said, 'Dear Counsellor, this is very strange sport, what can you mean by it?'

'Gracious me,' replied Drosselmeier, laughing, 'haven't you heard my watchmaker's song? I always sing it to such patients as Marie.' With this he drew his chair close to her bed, and said, 'Do not be angry that I did not pick out the Mouse King's fourteen eyes, it could not be done. But I have a surprise for you which I think you'll like.' With these words he slowly pulled something from his pocket. It was Nutcracker, with all his teeth and his jaw repaired.

Maria cried out for joy and her mother said, 'You see, Marie, Godfather Drosselmeier meant well by Nutcracker.'

'But you must confess, Maria,' said the Counsellor, 'that Nutcracker is hardly a handsome fellow. How this ugliness came to be hereditary in the family, I will now relate to you, if you will listen. Or perhaps you know already the story of the Princess Pirlipat and Lady Mouserings, and the skilful watchmaker?'

'But Godfather Drosselmeier,' interrupted Fritz, 'you have mended Nutcracker's teeth and his jaw, but where is his sword? Why have you not put on his sword?'

'Why must you be always meddling,' replied the Counsellor, angrily, 'I have cured Nutcracker's wounds, now it is up to him to find a sword.' The Counsellor turned to Marie. 'Tell me, have you heard the story of the Princess Pirlipat?'

'I hope this won't be one of your usual frightening tales, Counsellor,' said the mother.

'By no means, dear lady,' replied Drosselmeier, 'on the contrary, this one is rather amusing and merry.'

'Begin, begin, Godfather!' cried the children, and so the Counsellor began.

Pirlipat's mother was the wife of a king, and therefore a queen, which made Pirlipat a princess from the moment she was born. The king was beside himself with joy when he saw his daughter in her cradle, and he shouted, 'Was there ever anything more beautiful than my little Pirlipat?' And in truth, the world had never seen a lovelier child. Her complexion was as fair as a lily with rose-red flushes at her cheeks, her eyes were a sparkling azure and she had the most beautiful golden ringlets. Furthermore, she had been born with two rows of pearly white teeth, which she used to bite the High Chancellor when he was examining her features too closely. The whole kingdom rejoiced at such a sharp and clever princess.

Only the queen was uneasy and spent much of her time at the cradle. Nobody could understand why she insisted that the doors to the nursery were guarded by soldiers, and that six maids stay with the princess at night in addition to her two nurses. But strangest of all was the fact that each of these maids was ordered to keep a purring cat on their lap at all times during their watch. Nobody knew the reason for the queen's strange behaviour – but I know, children, and I shall explain.

It happened that some time before, many great kings and fine princes had assembled at the court of Pirlipat's father. It was a splendid affair and the king, determined to show that he had no want of gold or silver, resolved to hold an enormous banquet for his guests. Having been informed by the overseer of the kitchen that now was the time for the livestock to be slaughtered, he decided that a feast of sausages would be just fitting for the occasion.

'You know, my dear,' he said sweetly to the queen, 'how extremely fond I am of sausages.'

The queen knew at once that she was to undertake the task of making the sausages herself, as she had often done before. She ordered the Lord Treasurer to have the great golden sausage boiler and the silver chopping knives sent to the kitchen. A large fire of sandalwood was made, the queen put on her damask apron, and soon the sweet smell of sausage meat began to steam up out of the kettle.

The important moment had now arrived when the fat was to be chopped into little pieces, and browned gently in the silver stew-pans. The queen ordered her maids of honour to leave the kitchen, so that she might show her devotion to her husband by performing this task alone. But just as the fat began to sizzle, a tiny voice was heard:

'Give me a little of the fat, sister – I should like my part of the feast, since I am also a queen.'

The queen knew very well that the voice belonged to none other than Lady Mouserings. Lady Mouserings had lived in the palace these many years and maintained that she was related to the royal family. She also claimed that she was queen of a kingdom called Mousalia, which held its court under the hearth.

The queen was a kind lady, and although she was not willing to acknowledge Lady Mouserings as a true queen and sister, she was ready to allow her a small banquet on this great holiday. So she answered, 'You are welcome to a little of the fat, Lady Mouserings.'

Upon this, Lady Mouserings leaped out onto the hearth, and seized the fat the queen offered her with her little paws. But now, all the cousins and aunts of Lady Mouserings came running out to share in the feast. Finally, her seven sons appeared, who were so rude and unruly that they ran all over the fat and the terrified queen could not drive them away. Luckily, the chief maid of honour came in just at that moment and chased away the intruding guests, so that a little of the fat was left. The king's mathematician was summoned and he calculated that there was just enough to season the remaining sausages if distributed judiciously.

Drums and trumpets now heralded the start of the feast. The king was seated at the head of the table, smiling from ear to ear in anticipation of his sausages. The first course of sausage balls was brought in, and it was observed that as he ate the king grew pale and sighed gently every now and then. But in the second course, which consisted of the long sausages, he sank back upon his throne, sobbing and moaning with his head in his hands.

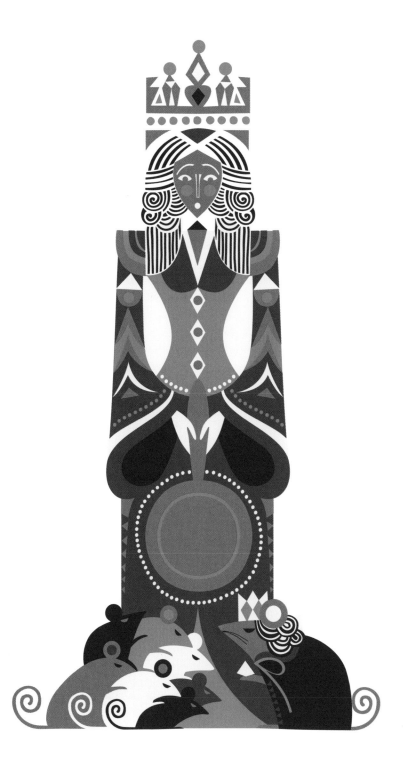

ll sprang up from the table in alarm and the royal physician was summoned. At last the king seemed to come to himself somewhat, and whispered in a voice that was barely audible, 'Too little fat!'

Then the queen threw herself in despair at his feet and sobbed, 'Oh, my poor husband! Alas! Lady Mouserings with her seven sons, and aunts and cousins, have eaten up the fat, and—'

'How has this happened?' interrupted the king and, full of rage, leaped to his feet.

Having heard the story, the king resolved to take vengeance upon Lady Mouserings and her family for having eaten up the fat of his sausages.

The Privy Council was called, and it was decided that Lady Mouserings was to be summoned to trial and all her estates confiscated. Worried that she might eat up more of his fat in the meantime, however, the king turned to the royal clockmaker and mechanist.

The clockmaker (whose name was Christian Elias Drosselmeier, the same as mine) came up with an unusual scheme to drive Lady Mouserings and her family from the palace forever. He invented several curious little machines, in which a piece of toasted fat was fastened to a thread. These Drosselmeier placed around Lady Mouserings' dwelling.

Lady Mouserings was much too wise to fall for such a trick, but despite all her warnings, every one of her seven sons, and many of her cousins and aunts, went into Drosselmeier's machines. As they tried to snatch the fat, an iron grating fell down behind them and they were trapped. They were then taken to the kitchen and slaughtered. Lady Mouserings, with the little remnant of her family, fled.

All the kingdom rejoiced. Only the queen was anxious, for she was sure that Lady Mouserings would not let the death of her sons go unavenged. And indeed one day, when the queen was in the kitchen preparing another of her husband's favourite dishes, Lady Mouserings appeared before her. 'My sons, my cousins and aunts are dead,' Lady Mouserings said. 'Take care, Queen, that Mouse Queen does not bite your little princess in two.' With this she disappeared and the queen was so frightened that she let the meat fall into the fire; and thus a second time Lady Mouserings spoiled a favourite dish for the king.

'But that is enough for tonight, children,' said Drosselmeier, 'I shall continue another night.'

As the Counsellor was leaving, Fritz cried, 'Did you really invent the mousetrap, Godfather Drosselmeier?'

The Counsellor smiled mysteriously, and said, 'Am I a skilful clockmaker yet unable to invent a mousetrap?'

'You know now, children,' commenced Coun-sellor Drosselmeier the following evening, 'why the queen was so carefully guarding Princess Pirlipat.'

Drosselmeier's machines were no protection against the wise Lady Mouserings, but the court astronomer declared that the family of Baron Purr would be able to keep Lady Mouserings from the cradle – and thus it came that every attendant must hold a cat upon her lap.

Late one night the two chief nurses started up out of a deep sleep. All around lay in quiet slumber and even the cats had ceased their purring. But what terror they felt as they saw before them a large, dreadful mouse, which stood erect upon its hind feet, and laid its ugly head against the face of the princess. With a cry they jumped up; all awoke, but in a moment Lady Mouserings (for the great mouse by Pirlipat's cradle was she) ran to the corner of the chamber. The cats leaped after her, but too late – she had disappeared through a hole in the floor.

Little Pirlipat awoke, crying at the noise. 'Thank heaven,' they cried, 'she lives!'

But how dreadful! When they looked at Pirlipat they saw what a change had come over the beautiful child. A large, ill-shaped head sat upon her shrivelled body, her azure blue eyes were changed into green staring ones, and her little mouth had stretched itself from ear to ear.

The queen nearly died from grief, and the king's library had to be lined with thick tapestry, for again and again he ran his head against the wall, crying out, 'Ah, me, unhappy monarch!'

He might now have seen how much better it would have been to eat his sausages without fat, and to leave Lady Mouserings and her family at peace under the hearth; but instead he laid all the blame upon the court watchmaker, Christian Elias Drosselmeier of Nuremberg.

He decreed that Drosselmeier must restore the Princess Pirlipat to her former condition within four weeks, or he should suffer a shameful death under the axe of the executioner. Drosselmeier was terrified, but he had great confidence in his skill and good fortune, and began immediately to take Princess Pirlipat apart. With great dexterity he unscrewed her little hands and feet, and carefully examined her insides; but he found, alas, that the princess would grow uglier as she grew bigger, and knew not what to do. He put the princess carefully together again, and sank down by her cradle in despair.

The fourth week had commenced when the king looked in with flashing eyes, and cried, 'Christian Elias Drosselmeier, cure the princess, or you must die.' Drosselmeier began to weep, but the Princess Pirlipat lay as happy as the day, and cracked nuts.

Pirlipat's appetite for nuts now struck the mechanist as uncommon, along with the fact that she had come into the world with teeth.

In truth, immediately after her transformation, she had screamed continually until a nut accidentally came her way, which she immediately put into her mouth, then cracked it, ate the kernel, and became calm. Since then her nurses made sure she was always supplied with nuts.

'Oh, sacred instinct of Nature!' cried Christian Elias Drosselmeier. 'You point me to the gates of this mystery. I will knock, and they will open.'

He begged straightaway to speak with the royal astronomer, and was led under guard to his apartment. They embraced with tears, for they had been warm friends, then retired to a private room and examined many books on instinct, sympathies, antipathies and other mysterious things.

Night came on; the astronomer looked at the stars, and set up the horoscope of Princess Pirlipat. It was a great deal of trouble, for the lines grew ever more intricate; but at last – what joy! – at last it became clear that the Princess Pirlipat, in order to be freed from the magic which had deformed her, had only to eat the kernel of the nut Crackatuck.

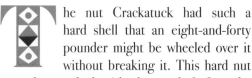

The nut Crackatuck had such a hard shell that an eight-and-forty pounder might be wheeled over it without breaking it. This hard nut must be cracked with the teeth before the princess, by a man who had never been shaved, and had never worn boots. The young man must then hand her the kernel with closed eyes, and must not open them again until he had marched seven steps backward without stumbling.

The king was seated at dinner on Sunday afternoon, when the mechanist, who was to have been beheaded early Monday morning, rushed in with joy and proclaimed that he had found a method of restoring to the Princess Pirlipat her lost beauty.

The king embraced him and promised him a diamond sword, four medals and two new Sunday suits.

'Immediately after dinner we will see to it, dear mechanist,' he added, 'that the unshorn young man in shoes is ready with the Crackatuck; and take care that he drinks no wine beforehand, for fear he should stumble as he goes the seven steps backward; afterward he may drink like a fish.'

Drosselmeier was most alarmed at these words; and, after much stammering, said that the nut Crackatuck and the young man to crack it were yet to be sought after – and that it was quite doubtful whether either would ever be found.

The king swung his sceptre about his crowned head, and roared with the voice of a lion, 'Then off goes your head!'

Fortunately for Drosselmeier the king's dinner was better than usual this day, so that he was disposed to listen to reason, while the good queen, moved by the hard fate of the mechanist, used her influence to soothe him. The king agreed at last that the watchmaker should leave the court instantly, accompanied by the royal astronomer, and never return without the Crackatuck in his pocket; and that the nutcracker be summoned by a notice in all the newspapers.

Here the Counsellor broke off again, promising to narrate the rest the following evening.

The next evening as soon as the candles were lit, Godfather Drosselmeier appeared, and continued his story:

Drosselmeier and the astronomer had been fifteen years on their journey without seeing any signs of the nut Crackatuck.

In the midst of a huge forest in Asia, Drosselmeier sank at last into despondency, suddenly desperate to see his dear native city, Nuremberg. 'Oh, sweet city,' he cried, 'where there are so many beautiful houses and windows!'

As Drosselmeier grieved, the astronomer was moved with sympathy, and began to howl pitifully. He soon composed himself, wiped the tears out of his eyes, and said: 'But, my respected colleague, why sit here and howl? Why should we not go to Nuremberg? Is it not the same, wherever we seek after this miserable Crackatuck?'

'That is true,' replied Drosselmeier, greatly consoled. Both arose, and went straight to Nuremberg.

As soon as they arrived, Drosselmeier ran to his brother, Christopher Zacharias Drosselmeier, puppet-maker and gilder, whom he had not seen for many years. The watchmaker told him the whole story of the Princess Pirlipat until he clapped with astonishment.

rosselmeier then told of his travels: how he had passed two years with the King of Dates, how coldly he had been received by Prince Almond, and how he had sought information of the Natural Society in Squirrelberg – in short, how his search to find even the least signs of the Crackatuck had been in vain.

During this account, Christopher Zacharias had often snapped his fingers, winked, tutted, and then called out: 'Hi – hem! – if it should!–'

At last, he clasped his brother round the neck, and cried: 'Brother, brother, you are safe! For I must be wonderfully mistaken if I have not that nut in my possession!' He then drew a little box from his pocket, and took out of it a gilded nut of moderate size. 'See,' he said, 'many years ago, a stranger came here at Christmas time with a sack full of nuts, which he offered for sale. Just as he passed my shop, he got into a fight with a nut-seller of this city. The man put his sack down, the better to defend himself, and at the same moment, a heavily laden wagon passed directly over it; all the nuts were cracked except this one, which the stranger, with a singular smile, offered me if I could give him a dollar dated 1720. I thought that strange, but as I found in my pocket just such a dollar, I bought the nut, and gilded it over, without knowing why I bought it, or why I set so much store by it.'

••••▲••••▲••••▲••••▲••••▲••••▲••••

All doubt whether this nut was actually the long-sought Crackatuck was instantly removed when the astronomer was called, who carefully scraped off the gold, and found engraved upon the rind the word 'Crackatuck'. The joy of the travellers was beyond bounds, and the brother the happiest man under the sun, for Drosselmeier assured him that his fortune was made, since he would have a considerable pension for the rest of his days.

The mechanist and the astronomer had both put on their night-caps, and were getting into bed as the latter said: 'My worthy colleague, good fortune never comes single. Take my word for it, we have found not only the Crackatuck, but also the young man who is to crack it. I mean your brother's son. I cannot sleep; no, this very night I must cast the youth's horoscope.' With these words, he threw the night-cap off his head, and began to take an observation.

The brother's son was in truth a handsome young man, who had never shaved nor worn boots. On Christmas days he wore a handsome red coat trimmed with gold, a sword, a hat under his arm, and a curling wig. In this fine dress he would stand in his father's shop, and out of gallantry crack nuts for the young girls, for which reason he was called the 'Nutcracker'.

••••▲••••▲••••▲••••▲••••▲••••▲••••

On the following morning the astronomer was in raptures: 'It is he — we have him — he is found! But there are two things we must do. Firstly, we must braid a stout wooden pole, which shall be joined to your nephew's lower jaw so that it can move it with great force. Next, when we arrive at the king's palace, we must let no one know that we have brought the young man with us who is to crack the Crackatuck. I read in his horoscope that after many young men have broken their teeth to no purpose, the king will promise to him who cracks the nut, and restores to the princess her lost beauty, the princess herself, and the succession to the throne as a reward.' His brother, the puppet-maker, was delighted to think that his son might marry the Princess Pirlipat, and become a prince, and he gave him up entirely into the hands of the two travellers.

The pole Drosselmeier fastened upon his hopeful nephew worked very well and he found he could crack even the hardest peach-stones.

As Drosselmeier and the astronomer had sent immediate news of their discovery of the Crackatuck to the palace, notices had been published, and when the travellers arrived, many handsome young men had appeared who, trusting to their sound teeth, were ready to undertake the disenchantment of the princess.

The travellers were horrified when they saw the princess again. Her little body, with its tiny hands and feet, was hardly able to carry her great misshapen head, and the ugliness of her face was increased by a white cotton beard, which had spread over her chin.

All was as the astronomer had read in the horoscope. One youth in shoes after another bit upon the nut Crackatuck until his teeth and jaws were sore, and were then led away, half swooning and sighing, 'That was a hard nut.'

After the king, in the anguish of his heart, had promised his daughter and his kingdom to him who should break the spell, the young Drosselmeier stepped forward, and begged for permission to try. No one had yet charmed Princess Pirlipat as much as young Drosselmeier; she laid her little hand upon her heart, and sighed, 'I hope he's the one to crack the Crackatuck and become my husband!' After young Drosselmeier had gracefully saluted the king and queen, and then the Princess Pirlipat, he received the Crackatuck, put it without hesitation between his teeth, pulled his pole very hard, and *crack* – the shell broke into many pieces. He then gave the kernel with a low bow to the princess, shut his eyes, and began to walk backwards. The princess straightaway swallowed the kernel, and behold! Her ugly shape was gone, and in its place appeared a most beautiful figure, with a face of roses and lilies, eyes of living, sparkling azure, and locks curling in bright golden ringlets.

rums and trumpets mingled with the loud rejoicings of the people. The king and his whole court danced, as at Pirlipat's birth, upon one leg; and the queen swooned from delight.

Young Drosselmeier was distracted by the tumult, but kept firm, and was just about to take the seventh step, when Lady Mouserings rose squealing out of the floor; down came his foot upon her head, and he stumbled and nearly fell.

Alas! What a hard fate! As quick as thought, his body shrivelled up and was hardly able to support his great misshapen head, his eyes turned green and staring, and his mouth was stretched from ear to ear. Instead of his pole, a narrow wooden cloak hung down upon his back, with which he moved his lower jaw.

The watchmaker and astronomer were benumbed with terror, while Lady Mouserings rolled bleeding and kicking on the floor.

Her malice did not go unpunished, for young Drosselmeier had trodden upon her neck so heavily with the heel of his shoe that she could not survive. When Lady Mouserings lay in her last agonies, she squeaked in a piteous tone:

'Oh, Crackatuck! Hard nut – hi, hi! – of thee I now must die! – que, que – son with seven crowns will bite – Nutcracker – at night – and avenge his mother's death – short breath – must I – hi, hi – die, die – so young – que, que – oh, agony! – queek!'

ith this cry, Lady Mouse-rings died, and the royal oven-heater carried out her body.

As for young Drosselmeier, no one troubled himself any further about him, but the princess reminded the king of his promise, and he commanded that the young hero be brought before him. But when the unfortunate youth approached, the princess held both hands before her face, and cried, 'Away, away with the ugly Nutcracker!' The court marshal took him by the shoulders, and pushed him out of doors. The king was full of anger, because the mechanist and astronomer had wished to give him a Nutcracker for a son-in-law, and he banished them forever from the kingdom.

This hadn't been in the horoscope but the astronomer was not discouraged. He immediately took another observation, and declared that he could read in the stars that young Drosselmeier would yet become a prince and a king; and that his former beauty would return, as soon as the son of Lady Mouserings, who had been born with seven heads, after the death of her seven sons, had fallen by his hand, and a maiden had loved him, notwithstanding his ugly shape. And they say that young Drosselmeier has actually been seen about Christmas time in his father's shop at Nuremberg, as a Nutcracker, it is true, but, at the same time, as a prince.

This, children, is the story of the Hard Nut; and you know now why people say so often, 'That was a hard nut to crack!' and whence it comes that Nutcrackers are so ugly.

The Counsellor thus concluded his story. Marie thought that the Princess Pirlipat was an ungrateful thing; and Fritz declared that if Nutcracker were anything of a man, he would not be long in settling matters with the Mouse King, and would get his old shape again very soon.

Whenever Marie tried to get up she felt dizzy, and she ended up having to stay in bed for a whole week; but at last she was well, and could play as merrily as ever. Everything in the glass case – the trees, flowers, houses, and beautiful dolls – looked as new and bright as ever. But, best of all, Marie found her dear Nutcracker again. He stood on the second shelf, and smiled at her with a good, sound set of teeth.

In the midst of the joy she felt in gazing at her favourite, a pang went through her heart when she thought of Godfather Drosselmeier's story – and she knew deep down that her Nutcracker could be none other than the young Drosselmeier of Nuremberg, Godfather Drosselmeier's enchanted nephew. That the watchmaker at the court of Pirlipat's father was Counsellor Drosselmeier himself, she did not doubt for an instant.

'But why didn't your uncle help you?' complained Marie, as it dawned on her that the battle she had seen was for Nutcracker's crown and kingdom. 'Is it not plain that the prophecy of the astronomer has been fulfilled, and that young Drosselmeier is prince and king of the puppets?'

While the shrewd Marie arranged all this so well in her mind, she believed, since she had seen it, that Nutcracker and his soldiers actually lived and moved. But everything in the glass case remained stiff and lifeless; yet Marie, far from giving up her conviction, cast all the blame on the magic of Lady Mouserings and her seven-headed son.

'But, even if you are not able to move, or to talk to me, dear Master Drosselmeier,' she said aloud to the Nutcracker, 'I know you understand me, and know what a good friend I am to you. You may depend upon my help, and I will beg of your uncle to bring his skill to your assistance, whenever you have need of it.'

Nutcracker remained still and motionless, but it seemed to Marie as if a gentle sigh was breathed in the glass case, so that the panes trembled and a voice rang out, like a little bell: ' Marie mine – I'll be thine – and thou mine – Marie mine!' Marie felt, in the cold shuddering that crept over her, a singular pleasure.

Twilight had come on; the doctor, with Godfather Drosselmeier, entered the sitting-room; and it was not long before all sat around for tea, talking cheerfully. Marie had seated herself at Godfather Drosselmeier's feet and, during a moment when they were all silent, she looked up at the Counsellor and said: 'I know, dear Godfather Drosselmeier, that my Nut-cracker is your nephew, and he has become a prince, or king rather, as the astronomer foretold. You know now that he is at war with the hateful Mouse King. Why do you not help him?'

Marie then related the whole course of the battle, just as she had seen it, and was often interrupted by the loud laughter of her mother and father. Only Fritz and Drosselmeier re-mained serious.

'here does the child get all this strange stuff in her head?' said the doctor.

'She has a lively imagination,' replied the mother; 'in fact, they are nothing but dreams caused by her violent fever.'

'That story is not true,' said Fritz. 'My red hussars are not such cowards as that. If I thought so — swords and daggers! — I would make a stir among them!'

But Godfather Drosselmeier, with a strange smile, took little Marie onto his lap, and said in a softer tone than he was ever heard to speak in before: 'Ah, dear Marie, more power is given to you than to me, or to the rest of us. You, like Pirlipat, were born a princess, for you reign in a bright and beautiful kingdom. But you will suffer if you take the part of the poor misshapen Nutcracker, for the Mouse King watches for him at every hole and corner. I cannot — you alone can rescue him; be firm and true.'

Neither Marie nor anyone else knew what Drosselmeier meant by these words; and they appeared so extraordinary to Doctor Stahlbaum that he felt the Counsellor's pulse, and said: 'Worthy friend, you have some violent congestion about the head; I will prescribe something for you.' But the mother shook her head thoughtfully, and spoke: 'I feel what it is that the Counsellor means, but I cannot express it in words.'

Not long after, Marie was woken one moonlit night by a strange rattling from a corner of the room. It sounded as if little stones were thrown; and every now and then there was a terrible squeaking.

'Ah! the mice – the mice are coming again!' exclaimed Marie, in fright. She was about to wake her mother but her voice failed her, and she could stir neither hand nor foot, for she saw the Mouse King work his way out of a hole in the wall, then run around and around the chamber, then jump up onto her bedside table.

'Hi – hi – hi – must give me thy sugar-plums – thy gingerbread – little thing – or I will bite thy Nutcracker – thy Nutcracker!' So squeaked the Mouse King, and snapped hideously with his teeth, then sprang down and away through the hole in the wall.

Marie looked very pale in the morning and was scarcely able to say a word. A hundred times she was going to tell her mother or Fritz what had happened, but she thought: 'No one will believe me, and I shall only be laughed at.'

This, at least, was very clear: that if she wished to save Nutcracker, she must give up her sugar-plums and her gingerbread. So, in the evening, she laid all that she had – and she had a great deal – at the bottom of the glass case.

The next morning, her mother said: 'It is strange what brings the mice all at once into the sitting-room. See, poor Marie, they have eaten all your gingerbread.'

And so it was. The ravenous Mouse King had not found the sugar-plums to his taste, but he had gnawed them with his sharp teeth, so that they had to be thrown away. Marie did not grieve about her cake and sugar-plums, for she was elated to think that she had saved the Nutcracker.

But what was her terror, when the very next night she heard a squealing close to her ear! The Mouse King was there again, and his eyes sparkled more dreadfully, and he squeaked much louder than before:

'Must give me thy sugar-puppets – chocolate figures – little thing – or I will bite thy Nut-cracker – thy Nutcracker!' and with this, the terrible Mouse King sprang down, and ran away. Marie was very sad; she went next morning to the glass case, and gazed sorrowfully at her sugar and chocolate figures.

And her grief was reasonable, for what beautiful figures little Marie Stahlbaum possessed! A pretty shepherd and shepherdess watched a whole flock of milk-white lambs; next came two letter-carriers, with letters in their hands; and then four neat pairs of nicely dressed boys and girls on a see-saw, white and smooth as marble; and lastly, in the corner, her darling – a tiny red-cheeked baby. And now the tears came into her eyes.

'h, dear Master Drosselmeier,' she said, turning to Nutcracker, 'there is nothing that I will not do to save you – but this is very hard!'

Nutcracker looked so miserable that Marie could imagine the Mouse King open his seven mouths to devour the unhappy youth; and she resolved to sacrifice them all. So that evening she put all her sugar figures at the bottom of the glass case. She kissed the shepherd, and the shepherdess, and the lambs, and at last took the red-cheeked baby out of the corner, and placed it down behind all the rest.

'Well, that is too bad!' said her mother, the next morning. 'All poor Marie's sugar figures are gnawed into pieces.' Marie could not keep from shedding tears, but she soon smiled again, and said to herself: 'That is nothing, if Nutcracker is only saved.'

In the evening, her mother told the Counsellor of the mischief the mouse had been doing: 'It is maddening that we cannot destroy this fellow that makes such havoc with Marie's sugar toys.'

'Ha!' cried Fritz, merrily. 'The baker opposite has a fine, grey cat; suppose I bring him over? He will soon have the mouse's head off.'

'And jump on the tables and chairs,' his mother laughed, 'and throw down cups and saucers, and do all kinds of mischief.'

'Ah, no,' said Fritz; 'the baker's cat is a light, careful fellow. I wish I could walk on a roof as well as he!'

'Fritz's plan is good,' said the doctor, 'but we will try a trap first. Have we got one?'

'Godfather Drosselmeier can make them best,' said Fritz, 'for he invented them.' All laughed; and, when the mother said that there was no mousetrap in the house, the Counsellor immediately sent for one and a very excellent mousetrap it seemed to be. The story of the Hard Nut now came vividly to the minds of the children. As the cook toasted the fat, Marie shook and trembled. Her head was full of the story and its wonders, and she said: 'Take care of Lady Mouserings and her family!' But Fritz had drawn his sword, and cried: 'Let them come on! I will scatter them!' But all remained still and quiet under the hearth. As the Counsellor tied the fat to a fine piece of thread, and set the trap softly, softly down by the glass case, Fritz cried out: 'Take care, Godfather Mechanist, or Mouse King will play you a trick!'

Ah, but what a night did Marie pass! Something cold as ice tapped against her arm; and crept, rough and hideous, across her cheek and squealed in her ear. The hateful Mouse King sat upon her shoulder. He opened his seven blood-red mouths, and, grating his teeth, he hissed:

'Wise mouse – wise mouse – goes not into the house – goes not to the feast – likes sugar things best – craft set at naught – will not be caught – give, give all – new frock – picture books – all the best – or shall have no rest – I will tear and bite – Nutcracker at night – hi, hi – que, que!'

arie looked very disturbed the following morning when Fritz told her that the mouse had not been caught, so that her mother thought she was grieving for her sugar things. 'Do not grieve, dear child,' she said; 'we will soon get rid of him. If the trap does not answer, Fritz shall bring his grey cat.'

As soon as Marie was alone in the sitting-room, she went to the glass case, and sobbed to Nutcracker: 'Ah, my dear, good Master Drosselmeier, what can I do? For, if I give up all my picture books, and even my new, beautiful dress, to the hateful mouse, he will ask more and more. And, when I have nothing left to give him, he will at last want me, instead of you, to bite in pieces.' As little Marie lamented, she saw a large spot of blood on Nutcracker's neck, which had been there ever since the battle. Now, since Marie found out that her Nutcracker was young Drosselmeier, the Counsellor's nephew, she did not carry him any more in her arms, nor hug and kiss him as she used to; indeed, she would very seldom touch him; but when she saw the spot of blood, she took him carefully from the shelf, and rubbed it with her handkerchief. But what was her astonishment, when she felt him suddenly grow warm in her hand, and begin to move! She put him quickly back on the shelf again, when — behold! — his little mouth began to work and twist, and at last, with a great deal of labour, he lisped out: 'Ah, dearest, best Miss Stahlbaum — excellent friend, how shall I thank you? No! No

picture books, no Christmas frock! – Get me a sword. For the rest, I–' Here speech left him, and his eyes, which had begun to express the deepest sympathy, became staring and motionless.

Marie did not feel the least terror; on the contrary, she leaped for joy, for she had now found a way to rescue Nutcracker without any more painful sacrifices. But where would she get a sword for him? Marie resolved to ask Fritz; and in the evening, when their parents had gone out, and they sat alone together by the glass case, she told him all that had happened to Nutcracker and Mouse King, and then begged him to furnish the little fellow with a sword. Fritz reflected long and earnestly on the poor account she gave him of the bravery of his hussars. He asked very seriously if it were really so. Marie assured him of it and Fritz ran to the glass case, addressed his hussars in a very moving speech, and then, as a punishment for their cowardice, cut their military badges from their caps. Then he turned to Marie: 'As to a sword, I can easily supply him with one. I yesterday permitted an old colonel to retire and consequently he has no further use for his fine sharp sabre.' The aforesaid colonel was living in the farthest corner of the third shelf. He was brought out and his silver sabre was taken from him and buckled about Nutcracker.

Marie could scarcely get to sleep that night, she was so anxious and fearful. About midnight, she heard a strange rustling, and rattling, and slashing, in the sitting-room.

ll at once, it went 'Squeak!'

'The Mouse King!' cried Marie, and sprang in her fright out of bed. All was still; but presently she heard a gentle knocking at the door, and a soft voice was heard: 'Worthiest, best, kindest Miss Stahlbaum, open the door without fear!'

Marie knew the voice of the young Drosselmeier, so she threw her frock about her, and opened the door. Little Nutcracker stood outside, with a bloody sword in his right hand, and a wax taper in his left. As soon as he saw Marie, he bent down on one knee, and said: 'You – you alone it was that filled me with knightly courage, and gave this arm strength to contend with the presumptuous foe who dared to disturb your slumber. The treacherous Mouse King is overcome; he lies bathed in his blood. Scorn not to receive the tokens of victory from a knight who will remain devoted to your service until death.' With these words, Nutcracker took off the seven crowns of the Mouse King, which he had hung on his left arm, and gave them to Marie, who joyfully received them. Nutcracker then arose, and said: 'Best, kindest Miss Stahlbaum, you know not what beautiful things I could show you at this moment while my enemy lies vanquished, if you would follow me for a few steps. Will you not be so good, Miss Stahlbaum?'

Marie consented to follow him, because she trusted him and was convinced that he would indeed show her many beautiful things. 'I will go with you, Master Drosselmeier,' she said; 'but it must not be long, for I have hardly had any sleep.'

'I will choose, then,' replied Nutcracker, 'the nearest, though more difficult way.' Marie followed him, until he stopped before a large, antique wardrobe in the hall. Marie perceived, to her astonishment, that the doors of the wardrobe, which were always kept locked, now stood wide open, so that she could see her father's fox-fur travelling coat. Nutcracker clambered nimbly up until he could grasp the tassel which hung down the back of the coat. As soon as he pulled the tassel, a little staircase of cedar-wood stretched down from the sleeve of the coat to the floor. 'Ascend, if you please,' cried Nutcracker.

Marie did so; but scarcely had she gone up the sleeve and seen her way out at the collar, when a dazzling light broke forth, and all at once she stood upon a sweet-smelling meadow, surrounded by millions of sparks, which darted up like flashing jewels. 'We are now in Candy Meadow,' said Nutcracker, 'but we will directly pass through yonder gate.' When Marie looked up, she saw the beautiful gate, which stood a few steps before them. It seemed built of marble; but when Marie came nearer, she saw that it was made of sugar, almonds and raisins, kneaded and baked together. On a gallery built over the gate were six apes in red jackets, who struck up the finest Turkish music which was ever heard. Soon the sweetest smells streamed around them, wafted from a small wood that opened on each side before them. Among the dark leaves, the golden and silvery fruit shone and sparkled, while the trunks and branches were ornamented with ribbons and flowers; and when the sweet perfume stirred and moved like a soft breeze, it rustled among the boughs and leaves like music, to which the dancing sparkles kept time!

'Ah, how delightful it is here!' cried Marie, entranced in happiness. 'We are in Christmas Wood,' said Nutcracker. 'Oh, if I could but linger here a while,' cried Marie. 'It is too, too charming!' Nutcracker clapped his hands, and some little shepherds and shepherdesses, and hunters and huntresses approached, who were so delicate and white that they seemed made of pure sugar. They brought a dainty armchair, all of gold, and invited Marie to sit down. She did so, and immediately the shepherds and shepherdesses danced a very pretty ballet, while the hunters blew their horns, and then all disappeared again into the bushes. They now walked along by a soft, rustling brook, out of which the scent of oranges seemed to arise and fill the whole wood.

his is the Orange Brook,' said Nutcracker, 'but it cannot compare either in size or beauty with Lemonade River.' Marie soon heard a louder rustling and dashing, and then saw the broad Lemonade River, which rolled in proud cream-coloured billows between banks covered with bright green bushes. A refreshing coolness arose from its waves. Nearby, a dark yellow stream dragged itself lazily along and smelled very sweet, and many little children sat on the shore angling for tiny fish, which were shaped like peanuts. At a distance there was a neat little village by the stream; houses, churches, parsonages and barns were all dark brown, with gilded rooves and sugar-plums stuck on the walls. 'That is Gingerbreadville,' said Nutcracker. 'The inhabitants are lovely-looking but rather grumpy because they suffer from toothache – and so we will not visit it.'

Then Marie saw a beautiful little town in which the houses were of bright translucent colours. Nutcracker went straight towards it, and now Marie heard a busy, merry clatter, and saw a thousand tiny figures collected around some heavily laden wagons, which had stopped in the market. From these they unloaded sheets of coloured paper and chocolate cakes. 'We are now in Bonbon Town,' said Nutcracker. 'The inhabitants are often terribly threatened by the armies of General Gnat, so they fortify their houses with stout materials from Paper Land, and throw up fortifications of the strong bulwarks, which King Chocolate sends to them.

But, worthiest Miss Stahlbaum, we will not visit all the little towns and villages of this land. To the capital!'

Nutcracker hastened on, and Marie followed, full of curiosity. It was not long before the smell of roses enveloped them, and everything around was touched with a soft rosy glow. Marie realised this was the reflection of a pink lake, which rippled before them, in little waves. Beautiful silver-white swans with golden collars swam and sang sweet tunes, while small diamond fish dipped up and down, as if dancing. 'Ah,' exclaimed Marie, ardently, 'this must be the lake which Godfather Drosselmeier was once going to make for me – and I myself am the maiden, who is to stroke the dear swans.'

Nutcracker laughed in a scornful manner, such as Marie had never observed in him before: 'Godfather Drosselmeier can never make anything like this. You – you yourself, rather, sweetest Miss Stahlbaum – but we will not trouble ourselves with that. Let us sail across the Rose Lake to the capital.'

Nutcracker clapped his hands again and the waves on Rose Lake rolled higher, and Marie saw in the distance a carriage made of shells, covered with sparkling jewels and drawn by two golden dolphins. Twelve little Moors, with caps and aprons braided of humming-bird's feathers, leaped upon the shore, and carried, first Marie, and then Nutcracker, with a gliding step, over the waves, and placed them in the carriage, which began to move across the lake. Ah, how delightful it was as Marie sailed along, with the rosy air and rosy waves breathing and dashing around her! The two dolphins raised up their heads, and spouted clear, crystal streams from their nostrils, high, high in the air, which fell down again in a thousand quivering, flashing rainbows, and it seemed as if two small silver voices sang out:

'Who sails upon the rosy lake? The little fairy – awake, awake! Music and song – bim-bim, fishes – sim-sim, swans – tweet-tweet, birds – whiz-whiz, breezes! – rustling, ringing, singing, blowing! – a fairy o'er the waves is going! Rosy billows, murmuring, playing, dashing, cooling the air! – roll along, along.'

Marie gazed into the rosy waves, out of which the face of a beautiful maiden smiled up at her. 'Ah!' she cried joyfully. 'Look, Master Drosselmeier! There is the Princess Pirlipat down in the water! Oh, how sweetly she smiles at me!'

utcracker sighed quite sorrowfully: 'Oh, kindest Miss Stahlbaum, that is not the Princess Pirlipat – it is you – it is your own lovely face that smiles so sweetly out of the Rose Lake.' At this, Marie drew her head back and blushed. Just then, she was lifted out of the carriage by the twelve Moors, and carried to the shore. They found themselves in a small thicket, more bright and sparkling even than Christmas Wood, with multi-coloured fruits hanging from the trees. 'We are now in Sweetmeat Grove,' said Nutcracker, 'but yonder is the capital.'

And what a sight! The beauty and splendour of the city before Marie's eyes was indescribable. The walls and towers glittered and the rooves of the houses were intricately braided crowns; and the towers were hung with the most beautiful garlands that ever were seen. As they passed through the gate, silver soldiers presented arms, and a little man in a brocade dressing-gown threw himself upon Nutcracker, with the words: 'Welcome, best prince! Welcome to Confectionville!'

Marie was astonished to hear young Drosselmeier called a prince by such a distinguished man. But she now heard such a hubbub of little voices, such a singing and playing, that she could think of nothing else, and turned to Nutcracker to ask him what it all meant. 'Oh, Miss Stahlbaum, it is nothing uncommon. Confectionville is a populous and merry city; thus it goes here every day. Let us walk farther, if you please.'

They had only gone a few steps, when they came to the great market-place, which was a wonderful sight. All the houses around were of sugared filigree work; gallery was built over gallery, and in the middle stood a tall obelisk of white and red sugared cream, while four fountains of lemonade and soda-water played in the air; and in the great basin were soft fruits, mixed with sugar and cream, and touched a little by the frost. But lovelier than all this were the charming little people, who, by the thousands, pushed and jested, and sang. Here were beautifully dressed men and women, soldiers, preachers, shepherds and harlequins – in short, all the people that can possibly be found in the world.

arie could not help crying out in wonder because they suddenly stood before a castle glimmering with rosy light, and crowned with a hundred airy towers. Beautiful bouquets of violets, narcissus, tulips and dahlias were hung about and their deep, glowing colours only heightened the dazzling, rose-white walls upon which they were fastened. The large cupola of the central building and the sloping rooves of the towers were spangled with a thousand gold and silver stars. 'We are now in front of Marchpane Castle,' said Nutcracker. Marie was lost in admiration, yet it did not escape her that one of the towers was without a roof, while little men were busied in repairing it on a scaffolding of cinnamon. 'Not long ago, this beautiful castle was threatened with serious injury, if not with entire destruction,' the Nutcracker continued. 'The Giant Sweet-tooth came this way, and bit off the roof of yonder tower, and was gnawing on it, when the people of Confectionville gave up to him a full quarter of the city, and a considerable portion of Sweetmeat Grove, with which he contented himself, and went on his way.'

At this moment soft music was heard, the doors of the palace opened, and twelve little pages marched out with lighted cloves, which they carried in their hands like torches.

ach of their heads was a pearl; their bodies were made of rubies and emeralds; and they walked upon feet of pure gold. Four ladies followed them, almost as tall as Marie's Clara, but so splendidly dressed that she knew they must be princesses. They embraced Nutcracker in the tenderest manner, and cried with joyful sobs: 'Oh, my best prince! Oh, my brother!'

Nutcracker seemed very much moved; he wiped the tears out of his eyes; then took Marie by the hand, and said with great emotion: 'This is Miss Marie Stahlbaum, the daughter of a much-respected physician, and my saviour. Had she not thrown her shoe at the right time – had she not supplied me with the sword of a pensioned colonel, I should now be lying in my grave, torn and bitten to pieces by the terrible Mouse King. Gaze upon her and tell me if Pirlipat, although a princess by birth, can compare with her in beauty, goodness and virtue?'

And all the ladies cried out 'No!' and then threw their arms around Marie, exclaiming: 'Ah, dear saviour of the prince, our beloved brother! Charming Miss Marie Stahlbaum!' She now accompanied these ladies and Nutcracker into the castle, and entered a room that was full of little chairs, sofas and bureaus made of brazilwood, ornamented with golden flowers, and had walls of bright-coloured crystal. The princesses brought out little cups and saucers, and plates and dishes, all of the finest porcelain. Then they brought the finest fruits and sugar-things, and began to prepare a delicious meal. Marie wished she could assist the princesses – and the most beautiful of Nutcracker's sisters, as if she had guessed Marie's secret thoughts, handed her a little golden mortar, saying: 'Oh, sweet friend, will you not pound some of this sugar-candy?'

While Marie worked, Nutcracker began to give a full account of his adventures – of the dreadful battle between his army and that of the Mouse King, and how he had lost it by the cowardice of his troops; how the terrible Mouse King lay in wait to bite him in pieces, and how Marie, to preserve him, gave up many of his subjects, who had entered her service, and all just as it had happened. During this narration, it seemed to Marie as if his words became less and less audible, and the pounding of her mortar also sounded more and more distant, until she could scarcely hear it; presently, she saw a silver gauze before her, in which the princesses, the pages, Nutcracker and herself were all enveloped. A singular humming and rustling and singing was heard, which seemed to die away in the distance; and now Marie was raised up, as if upon mounting waves, higher and higher – higher and higher – higher and higher!

And then Marie was falling, falling, falling when – poof! She opened her eyes and found herself in her own bed. Light flooded the room, and her mother was standing over her saying, 'How can you have slept so long? Breakfast has been ready for a long while.'

You have probably gathered, readers, that Marie, overwhelmed by the wonderful things she had seen, had finally fallen asleep in the room at Marchpane Castle, and that the Moors, or the pages, or perhaps even the princesses themselves had carried her home and put her to bed.

'Mama, you will not believe the things young Master Drosselmeier showed me last night!' And she told her mother the whole story as you have just heard it, whilst her mother listened in astonishment. When she had finished, her mother said: 'You have been dreaming, my dear, but now put it out of your mind.'

As Marie insisted that she had not been dreaming but had really seen those marvellous things, her mother led her to the glass case in the sitting-room, took Nutcracker from his usual spot on the second shelf and said: 'Silly child, how can you believe that this little doll could come to life?'

'But Mama,' replied Marie, 'little Nutcracker is young Master Drosselmeier of Nuremberg. He is Godfather Drosselmeier's nephew.'

When this was met with peals of laughter from her parents, Marie ran into the other chamber, retrieved the seven crowns of the Mouse King from her little box, brought them in, and handed them to her mother. 'Look Mama, here are the seven crowns of the Mouse King, which young Master Drosselmeier gave me last night as a token of his victory.' Her mother examined the little crowns in astonishment; their sheen was so bright and strange, and they were so delicately worked, that it seemed impossible that mortal hands could have formed them. Her father was equally astounded and insisted very sternly that Marie confess how she had obtained them. But Marie kept firm to her story so her father spoke very harshly to her and even called her a little story-teller, at which point she began to cry bitterly.

At this moment the door opened and Counsellor Drosselmeier entered.

'What's all this?' he exclaimed. Doctor Stahlbaum told him of all that had happened, and showed him the crowns. As soon as the Counsellor cast his eyes on them, he laughed and cried: 'Stupid pack – stupid pack! These are the very crowns I used to wear on my watch chain and which I gave to little Marie on her second birthday.'

arie ran to Godfather Drossel-meier, crying, 'Tell them, God-father, tell them that my Nutcracker is your nephew, young Master Drosselmeier of Nuremberg, and that it was he who gave me the crowns!'

But the Counsellor became grave and mut-tered: 'Stuff and nonsense!'

Doctor Stahlbaum then drew Marie onto his knee and said very seriously: 'Listen to me, Marie. If you don't put this foolish nonsense out of your head once and for all, I shall throw all of your dolls out of the window, Nutcracker and Miss Clara included'

So poor Marie did not dare speak further of her adventures, but she thought about them continuously. She found that if she concentrated very hard, she could make those wonderful visions reappear before her eyes. Therefore, instead of playing as she used to, she now sat quiet and reflective, lost in her thoughts. She was often scolded for this, and called a 'little daydreamer'.

It happened some time afterward that the Counsellor had come to the home of Dr Stahlbaum to repair one of the clocks in the sitting-room. As he worked, Marie sat close by the glass case gazing at Nutcracker, when all of a sudden she cried, quite without knowing what she was saying, 'Oh, if you were living, Master Drosselmeier, I would not slight you for sacrificing your beauty for my sake, as Princess Pirlipat did.'

Just then there was a loud knocking at the door. Counsellor Drosselmeier shouted, 'Hey – hey – stupid pack!' and Marie almost fell off her chair with fright.

'Marie,' her mother said from the doorway. 'This is Godfather Drosselmeier's nephew just arrived from Nuremberg.'

Counsellor Drosselmeier was holding by the hand a small but finely built young man with a complexion as fair as milk and cheeks as red as blood. He wore a very handsome red coat trimmed with gold, brightly polished shoes and silk stockings, and he carried a sword by his side, which sparkled and flashed so brightly that it might have been made of diamonds. It was obvious that he was an extremely polite and well-bred young man, for he had brought a great many thoughtful gifts – sweet gingerbread and some sugar figures for Marie, and a marvellous sabre for Fritz. At dinner he cracked nuts for the whole company – even the hardest were no object to him. He merely put one into his mouth, gave his long pigtail a pull and – *crack* – out popped the kernel. After dinner, he asked Marie to go with him into the sitting-room, and she blushed deeply.

Scarcely were they alone when young Drosselmeier fell on one knee, and said: 'Oh, lovely Miss Stahlbaum, you see here at your feet the happy Drosselmeier, whose life you saved on this very spot. You said that you would not slight me as the unkind Pirlipat did, and from that moment I ceased to be a miserable Nutcracker, and resumed again my former figure. Miss Stahlbaum, please do me the honour of giving me your hand in marriage. Please share with me crown and kingdom and rule with me in Marchpane Castle, for there I am still king!'

Marie accepted at once, and after one year and a day he arrived to carry her away in a golden chariot drawn by silver horses. The wedding, they say, was quite a magnificent spectacle with twenty-two thousand dancers dressed up with pearls and diamonds. Marie still reigns there, queen of sparkling Christmas woods and the wonderful Marchpane Castle. Like Marie, you can find all manner of wonderful things there, if you only take the time to look.

The End

ERNST THEODOR AMADEUS HOFFMANN was one of the most important writers of German Romanticism. He is probably best remembered for his novellas and short stories, which combine fantastical elements with a darker realism and examine the harmful effect of the unfettered imagination on the pathological mind. His novella *The Sandman* inspired Delibes' ballet *Coppelia*, whilst *The Nutcracker and the Mouse King* became the basis of Tchaikovsky's much-loved Christmas ballet.

SANNA ANNUKKA spent her childhood summers in Finland, and its landscape and folklore remain a source of inspiration. A print maker and illustrator based in Brighton, she is also a designer for Finnish textile brand Marimekko and has been featured in *Vogue* and many interior design magazines. She has also illustrated *The Fir Tree* and *The Snow Queen* by Hans Christian Andersen.

The Fir Tree

HANS CHRISTIAN ANDERSEN

Illustrated by

SANNA ANNUKKA

The Snow Queen

HANS CHRISTIAN ANDERSEN

Illustrated by

SANNA ANNUKKA